THE PRINCESS AND THE PIRATE

A.M. Luzzader

Illustrated by Anna M. Clark

Published by Knowledge Forest Press
P.O. Box 6331
Logan, UT 84341

Ebook ISBN-13: 978-1-949078-69-5
Paperback ISBN-13: 978-1-949078-68-8

Cover design by Sleepy Fox Studio, www.sleepyfoxstudio.net

Editing by Chadd VanZanten

Interior illustrations by Anna M. Clark, annamclarkart.com

The real-life Princess Olivia and Princess Juniper

CONTENTS

CHAPTER ONE
A DAY AT THE BEACH

THIS IS A FANTASY STORY. As you know, lots of fantasy stories begin with, "Once upon a time..."

This one doesn't begin that way.

That's because the story wasn't just "once upon a time." It was on a Saturday. And so this story will begin with "Once upon a Saturday..."

Once upon a Saturday, there was a place called Wildflower Kingdom. In Wildflower Kingdom, there was a castle. Inside the castle, there lived a royal family.

The queen of the family was named Jennifer. She had long, brown hair. She enjoyed eating licorice and reading books, but not always at the same time. The king was named Andrew. He had a thick, black beard.

He enjoyed studying lakes, rivers, and waterfalls. Queen Jennifer and King Andrew had two daughters. Their names were Princess Olivia and Princess Juniper.

Princess Olivia was the older sister. She was eight years old. She loved foxes, gymnastics, chocolate-chip cookies, and unicorns.

Princess Juniper was the younger sister. She was six years old. She loved puppies, football, strawberries, and unicorns.

Queen Jennifer

King Andrew

Princess Olivia

Princess Juniper

Juniper and Olivia were very lucky because there were lots of unicorns in Wildflower Kingdom. There were hundreds of unicorns in Wildflower Kingdom. They feasted on the plentiful green grass that grew on the hill sides and in the valleys.

Wildflower Kingdom got its name from the many wildflowers that grew all throughout the land. There were many other beautiful parts of Wildflower Kingdom. For example, they could have named the kingdom the Fantastic Forest, because the castle was surrounded by a forest that was home to birds, squirrels, and even bears. The pine and aspen trees there were tall and strong and smelled lovely. Through the forest there was a path with a bridge that went over a small stream.

Wildflower Kingdom also could have been named Kindness Kingdom because the people that lived in Wildflower Kingdom were very kind to each other. One day, Princess Olivia once lost a mitten on her way to Wildflower Village. The villagers helped her look for it. The mitten was finally found in front of the little cafe on the corner.

On another day, Princess Juniper didn't just lose a mitten, she lost herself! She didn't know the way home, but some ladies in the village noticed she looked upset and so they helped her find her way back to the castle. In Wildflower Kingdom, the people smiled and said hello and tried to help each other. Kindness Kingdom would have been a very good name for the village.

Yes, there were lots of names that the Kingdom could have had, but Wildflower Kingdom was the name they had chosen. But even though that was the kingdom's name, there were some parts of it that didn't have wildflowers.

In fact, on this particular Saturday, Princess Olivia and Princess Juniper had gotten up very early in the morning. Princess Jennifer told them if they finished all their chores, they could go to the beach for a picnic lunch.

The beach was on the north side of the kingdom. The beach didn't have any wildflowers. Instead it had lots of sand and beach grass. The ocean waves swept in and out. The sun shone brightly and seagulls flew overhead.

The two princesses put on their swimsuits and spent most of the morning playing in the ocean. They squished sand between their toes. They jumped into the waves and swam.

They built a sandcastle and pretended it was Wildflower Castle, using small stones and seashells to decorate it. Then they went swimming again.

At lunchtime, the princesses changed back into their dresses. Then they joined their mother, Queen Jennifer, on a big blanket to eat some lunch.

"Miss Beets made us some delicious peanut butter sandwiches," said Queen Jennifer.

Miss Beets was the castle's head chef.

"And she packed some pickles," said Olivia. "I like pickles!"

"And she made a peach pie!" said Juniper.

They ate the sandwiches and the pickles and the pie. They all agreed that Miss Beets was an excellent chef.

When they had finished, Queen Jennifer said, "After lunch we will go to the harbor. We're meeting my big brother, Pirate Pete. He hasn't visited since you girls were very young. He has been on a long sea voyage searching for lost treasure. Do you remember him?"

Juniper and Olivia shook their heads. "No," they said.

"Ah, then it will be fun for you to see him again," said Queen Jennifer. "He will arrive on his ship at the harbor."

"Is it a pirate ship?" asked Olivia.

"I suppose it is," replied Queen Jennifer.

"I thought so," said Olivia.

"Why don't you girls go and make sure we haven't left any garbage behind," said Queen Jennifer. "I'll put our things away. Then we'll go to the harbor."

The two princesses walked around, looking carefully at the sand. Princess Juniper found an old bottle cap and a candy wrapper. Princess Olivia found a paper plate and an old tin can. It was not their litter, but they picked it up anyway. The beach was so pretty, they would never want to leave any trash behind. Now there was no litter or trash on the beach. There was only sand, beach grass, and sea shells.

Princess Olivia picked up a stick and wrote in the sand, *Have a lovely day! Love, the Princesses Olivia and Juniper.*

"I wonder what Pirate Pete is like," said Juniper. "I can't wait to meet him. I've never met a real pirate."

"I don't want to meet him," said Olivia. "Don't you know what a pirate is?"

Juniper thought about it for a moment. "I guess not," she said.

Olivia was older than Juniper. There were lots of things that Olivia knew that Juniper didn't know yet.

Olivia knew how to add very big numbers together. Juniper could only add smaller numbers together.

Olivia knew how to make a whole frozen pizza in the oven. Juniper could only make frozen waffles in the toaster.

"What is a pirate?" asked Juniper.

"Pirates are mean," said Olivia.

"Oh, my," said Juniper. Her eyes got big.

"Pirates sail the oceans in pirate ships and attack other ships," said Olivia.

"Oh, dear," said Juniper. Her mouth was wide open.

"Pirates steal treasure!" cried Olivia.

"Oh, no!" said Juniper. She put her hands on her cheeks.

Then Juniper remembered something. It was last year. She was visiting her cousin Prince Stewart in Rose Petal Kingdom, which was next door to Wildflower Kingdom. Juniper brought along one of her stuffed teddy bears. It was the teddy bear she called Timmy. Timmy had a tiny blue bow tie, and Juniper loved him very much.

However, Prince Stewart, who was about her age, had taken Timmy from Juniper without asking. Stewart wouldn't give Timmy back, not even when Juniper asked nicely. She finally had to tell her father. King Andrew talked to Stewart, and only then did Stewart finally give Timmy back to Juniper.

"So, Cousin Stewart is a pirate?" said Juniper with a frown on her face.

"What did you say?" asked Olivia.

"Nothing," mumbled Juniper. "Pirates don't sound very nice."

"Oh, they're not," said Olivia. "They can be quite ruthless."

"What's 'ruthless'?" asked Juniper.

"It means they don't care about other people," replied Olivia.

"If Pirate Pete is ruthless, I don't want to meet him," said Juniper.

Olivia shrugged. "He's our uncle. We should at least meet him."

Juniper didn't know what to think. Would Pirate Pete attack Wildflower Kingdom with his pirate ship? Would he be ruthless? Would Pirate Pete steal Timmy the teddy bear?

Just then, the two princesses heard their mother calling them. "Girls! Let's go to the harbor!"

"Well," whispered Juniper to herself, "I guess it's time to go and meet Pirate Pete."

CHAPTER TWO

A PIRATE AND A PIRATE SHIP

Queen Jennifer led Princess Olivia and Princess Juniper to the harbor. The harbor was a place where boats could come to shore when visiting Wildflower Kingdom. The harbor was protected from big ocean waves and storms. In the harbor, there was a dock. The dock was a long wooden walkway where ships could stop.

Overhead, seagulls called and flew on the breeze. Soon a great wooden sailing ship came into sight. It was built from wood, and its massive sails were white. The ship sailed toward the dock.

"Pirate ships have a black flag with a skull and crossbones," Olivia whispered to Juniper.

"That sounds scary," Juniper whispered to Olivia.

"I don't see a pirate flag on that ship," said Olivia.

"You sure know a lot about pirates," said Juniper nervously.

Olivia smiled. She liked to know lots of things.

As the ship got closer, the sailors on the ship brought down the sails. Some of them jumped off the ship and tied the ship to the dock with heavy ropes. Then the sailors laid a sort of bridge from the ship to the dock so that everyone could get off the boat. This was called a gangway.

A jolly man with a big red beard strolled down the gangway to the dock. He was very tall with broad shoulders. On his head he wore a wide, three-cornered hat.

His long black coat reached down to his knees. It had brass buttons and gold trim. Over one of the man's eyes there was a black eye patch. One of his legs wasn't a leg at all, but a wooden peg. And on his shoulder there sat a big parrot with feathers of green and red and yellow.

Even without asking, the princesses knew this was Pirate Pete.

"Ahoy!" shouted Pirate Pete, with a big grin. His voice was loud and deep, and his wooden peg made a loud *thump, thump, thump* on the gangway.

"What does *ahoy* mean?" Juniper asked Olivia.

"That's pirate-talk!" whispered Olivia.

"Oh, gosh," said Juniper, hiding herself behind Queen Jennifer.

"Pirate Pete! My brother!" exclaimed Queen Jennifer. "I'm so glad you could visit!"

"Queen Jennifer," said Pirate Pete with a bow. "It's always a pleasure to visit Wildflower Kingdom. Oh, my stars! Are these the princesses?"

"Yes," said Queen Jennifer. "They've grown so much since you've seen them. This is Princess Olivia and Princess Juniper. Girls, this is my brother. He's also your uncle, Pirate Pete."

Olivia gave Pirate Pete a little curtsy, but Juniper

only hid behind her mother.

"Well, I'm pleased to see you again, princesses. You were only little babies when I last came to your kingdom. You may call me Uncle Pete, and this is my parrot, Patty."

"Pretty bird, pretty bird," squawked the parrot.

Juniper thought Patty was indeed very pretty, but she tried to stay hidden.

"Queen Jennifer, I got the letter you sent to me.

You said you needed help with a treasure map?" asked Pirate Pete.

"Yes," said Queen Jennifer. "I have a mysterious treasure map. You're an expert with treasure maps, so I hope you can help us find the treasure."

The map was made of heavy brown paper. It was rolled up into a scroll. Queen Jennifer gave the map to Pirate Pete.

Pirate Pete unrolled it and held it up. He turned the map this way and that. "Hmm," he said. "Most interesting."

"Can you help us?" said Queen Jennifer.

"Aye," said Pirate Pete, nodding his head slowly.

"What does *aye* mean?" Juniper whispered to Olivia.

"More pirate-talk!" whispered Olivia.

"Aye, I can help you find the treasure," said Pirate Pete. "If we all work together, I think we can find the treasure before sundown!"

"I was hoping you would say that!" said Queen Jennifer.

"You want *us* to help?" asked Olivia.

"If you'd like to," said Pirate Pete in a friendly voice. "I've done lots of treasure hunting, and it's always easier and a lot more fun when people work together."

"I'll come along to help," said Queen Jennifer.

"And what about you princesses?" asked Pirate Pete.

"It's okay if you don't want to," said Queen Jennifer. "We can take you back to the castle and you can stay with your father."

Princess Olivia thought about it. Was he a mean pirate? She didn't want to help a mean pirate. But

Pirate Pete seemed nice, and Olivia had never been on a real treasure hunt before.

And so Princess Olivia nodded her head. "Yes, I'll help find the treasure," she said.

Princess Juniper thought about what Olivia said about pirates. Even though Pirate Pete seemed friendly, Juniper was still a bit afraid. But she had never been on a real treasure hunt, either. It sounded fun.

And so Princess Juniper stepped out from behind Queen Jennifer. "I'll help, too," she said shyly.

"Gold coins! Gold coins!" squawked Patty.

Pirate Pete laughed at Patty. "We don't know just what we'll find, Patty! Gold coins are splendid, but there are many kinds of treasure. Let me fetch my treasure-hunting tools from the ship, and we'll be on our way!"

The two princesses wondered what kinds of adventure they would see that day. No one noticed the sly smile on Queen Jennifer's face. The princesses didn't know it yet, but everything was going exactly how the queen had planned.

CHAPTER THREE

A MAP, A COMPASS, AND SOMETHING SCARY

Pirate Pete went to his ship and brought back a shovel, a lantern, and a compass. Then they spread out the map on the dock and looked at it.

"Where did you get this map anyway?" Pirate Pete asked Queen Jennifer.

Queen Jennifer smiled. "Oh, it just turned up. It's very mysterious."

It was a map of Wildflower Kingdom.

Juniper peeked over Pirate Pete's shoulder. "Hey, that's Wildflower Castle," she said, pointing at the map. "There's the path through the forest, and there's the village."

Olivia looked at the map, too. She pointed and said, "I see the bridge over the stream, and the beach."

"You two are quite right," said Pirate Pete, nodding his head. "And lookie here! A dotted red line! It starts here at the dock and leads down the beach. That will lead us to the treasure!"

He turned to Queen Jennifer. "Do you know what type of treasure it is? Is it gold coins or jewelry or ancient artifacts?"

"I'm not sure," said Queen Jennifer. "I guess we'll just have to wait and see."

"Only one way to find out, then," said Pirate Pete. "Let's go find that treasure!"

Olivia had nearly forgotten that Pete was a pirate. "Yeah," she said with a laugh. "Let's go!"

Juniper had not forgotten. She was still worried that Pirate Pete would be ruthless. But she was also curious about the treasure, so she went along.

"Princess Juniper," said Pirate Pete, "will you carry the map for us?"

"Um, sure," said Juniper nervously.

Pirate Pete gave Juniper the map. He also gave her a compass, which is a little device with a magnetic needle inside that always points north.

"With the map and compass," said Pirate Pete, "you can tell us which direction to go."

Pirate Pete carried the shovel and a small lantern.

"Old treasure is often buried or hidden in caves," said Pirate Pete. "That's why I always bring a shovel and a lantern."

Queen Jennifer smiled. Because it was such a sunny day, she carried a parasol, which is a big umbrella used to provide shade. Olivia and Juniper walked beneath the shade of the parasol, but Pete said he liked the sun.

The four of them walked down the beach while the sea birds circled and cried out above them. Juniper carefully kept one fingertip on the map to mark where they were. The dotted red line led them down the beach, but then it started to curve to the east. They followed the dotted red line. Pirate Pete stopped now and then to figure out which way to go. The dotted red line led up a hill, across a grassy field, and to a rocky cliff.

Suddenly, Juniper stopped walking. "The dotted red line keeps going," she said, "but there's a cliff here. How can we go into the cliff?"

Pirate Pete took off his hat and scratched his head. Where should they go next? He looked around. He searched along the cliff. He looked behind the rocks and bushes.

Then, Pirate Pete pointed and shouted, "Lookie here!"

Pirate Pete had found the dark opening of a cave hidden behind some bushes on the rocky cliff.

"This cave is where the map is leading us," said Pirate Pete. He stepped into the cave. Olivia and Queen Jennifer followed, but Juniper stayed outside.

Pirate Pete stepped back out of the cave and stood

by Juniper. "Don't you want to come with us?" he asked.

"Caves are dark and scary," said Juniper. "There could be bats or spiders inside!"

Pirate Pete scratched his scruffy red beard. "True, true," he said.

"Bats and spiders! Bats and spiders!" squawked Patty.

"But on the other hand," said Pirate Pete, "if we are careful, the cave could be interesting to explore. It will also be nice and cool inside, instead of hot like it is out here. Best of all, we might find a clue to find the treasure."

Princess Juniper wrinkled her brow. "Hmm," she said.

"It's up to you," said Pirate Pete. "I'll understand if you don't want to go in. You can always try it out, and if you don't like it, you can come back outside."

Juniper liked the sound of that. If she could change her mind later, going into the cave wasn't so scary. Besides, she wanted to find the treasure!

"Okay," said Juniper. "I'll go in, but I'll leave if I get too scared."

"Of course," said Pirate Pete. "I'm proud of you for being brave."

"Me, too," said Queen Jennifer. "Sometimes it's good to try things, even if you're a little bit afraid."

"Me too! Me too!" squawked Patty.

Olivia was actually looking forward to going into the cave. She would have gone in even if there wasn't a treasure. Olivia liked going on adventures and seeing new things.

Pirate Pete lit his lantern and everyone walked into the cave. It was dark inside. Juniper blinked her eyes and then opened them wide to see better. There was something on the wall next to her. Juniper turned to get a better look. Then, in the light of Pirate Pete's lantern, she saw it—it was a giant, hairy, terrifying spider!

CHAPTER FOUR

THE DEEP DARK CAVE

JUNIPER SQUEALED WITH FRIGHT. She turned, closed her eyes, and buried her face in the folds of Queen Jennifer's dress. Then she shouted, "I want to go home! I want to go home!"

Queen Jennifer knelt down and gave Juniper a hug. "What is it, dear? What's the matter?"

"I saw a giant spider!" she cried. "I saw a giant spider and I want to go home now!"

"Where?" said Pirate Pete. He held up his lantern. "Where's the giant spider? I'll make sure it doesn't come close!"

Juniper opened one eye and looked around the cave. She saw the spider. It wasn't giant. It wasn't very scary, either. In fact, it seemed more afraid than

Juniper was. It had run up the wall and was hiding in a crack in the rock.

"Oh," said Juniper. She pointed at the spider. "There it is. It looked a lot bigger at first."

"Would you like to go back out of the cave?" said Pirate Pete. "Or would you like to continue?"

Juniper thought about it. "Do you think there will be any spiders bigger than that one?"

"Possibly," said Pirate Pete. "We can't know for sure. You can always leave if we find a really big one."

"Okay," said Juniper, taking Queen Jennifer's hand. "Let's continue."

As they went deeper into the dark cave, Princess Juniper was glad that she had stayed with the others. Even if she was a little scared, the cave was very interesting. The walls sparkled with cave crystals. They saw a few other spiders, but they all just scurried away. It was also nice and cool inside.

"The cave is cooler because part of it is underground," said Pirate Pete. "Because the air inside the cave is colder, it flows out. It is like the cave is breathing."

Soon Princess Juniper let go of Queen Jennifer's hand and ran ahead. She wanted to see more of the cave.

"Come on, Olivia," said Juniper. To her surprise, her voice echoed back from the cave.

"*Come on, Olivia,*" said the echo.

Olivia noticed the echo and she tried it, too. She cupped her hands at her mouth and shouted, "Woo woo!"

"*Woo woo!*" answered the echo.

"Patty was copying everything we said, and now the cave is too!" cried Juniper.

"The cave is too! The cave is too!" squawked Patty.

"*The cave is too! The cave is too!*" answered the echo.

Pirate Pete's lantern guided the way.

"Take a look at that map, girls," said Pete. "See if you can find where we're supposed to go."

"The dotted red line turns down this way and leads to a big round rock," said Olivia, looking at the map, and then pointing into the cave.

Pirate Pete held up his lantern. They went forward and came to a giant round rock.

"Here's the round rock!" said Pirate Pete. "Now what?"

"It says to take ten giant steps in this direction,"

said Juniper, looking closely at the map. "But then the red dotted line just stops, and there's a big X."

"Yo ho ho!" cried Pirate Pete.

"Is that more pirate-talk?" Juniper whispered to Olivia.

Olivia closed her eyes and nodded wisely.

"The big X!" shouted Pirate Pete. "That's where the treasure must be!"

"Let's hurry," said Queen Jennifer with a smile.

They all took ten more steps, but there was nothing there.

"Don't dawdle now," said Pirate Pete, looking all around the cave. "The treasure is close by!"

"But there's nothing here," said Juniper. "Where's the treasure?"

"It must be a buried treasure," said Pirate Pete. "This is where we dig. We'll all take turns."

Now Olivia frowned. "I don't want to dig."

"Why not?" asked Queen Jennifer.

"Because it will take a long time," said Olivia. "I'll get dirty and tired. And my dress will get messy!"

Pirate Pete pushed his hat back on his head. "True, true. It may take a long time. And we might get a bit dirty. But if we all help, it might not be so bad. Anything worth having is worth putting in a bit of work for, wouldn't you agree?"

Olivia shrugged.

"Would you be willing to try digging for a few minutes?" asked Pirate Pete.

Olivia thought about it. Digging a hole sounded rather like a chore. She already had done lots of chores before they came to the beach. She would have preferred if they had found a treasure chest without having to dig.

"Maybe you could even find a way of making it fun," said Pirate Pete.

"Okay," said Olivia. "I'll try."

So the group started digging. Juniper took the first turn because she was the most excited to find the treasure, and she enjoyed playing in the dirt. Because she was so young, Juniper found the shovel to be very heavy. So even though she enjoyed digging in the dirt, she had to let someone else have a turn after only a couple minutes.

Pirate Pete went next. He was able to scoop up great loads of dirt.

"The treasure must be very deep," said Princess Olivia.

Pirate Pete was shoveling a lot more dirt than Juniper had but after a few minutes, he wiped his brow. "Whew," he said. "I think I need a break. Olivia, do you want to shovel?"

Princess Olivia was still worried that it would be hard work and would be tiring. After all, both Juniper and Pete were already tired. Still, if it helped get them the treasure, she was willing to try.

Olivia took the shovel and dug up a shovel load of

dirt. The shovel was heavy and there was a lot of dirt around. But to Olivia's surprise, it was actually kind of fun. She liked the sound the shovel made when it hit the dirt, and with each shovel she tried to see how much dirt she could balance on the shovel. It was a little bit like a game!

"You're right," said Olivia. "Digging for treasure is fun!"

Olivia was just about to try for her biggest shovel of dirt, but when the shovel hit the dirt it made a strange thud.

"That must be the treasure!" said Pirate Pete, his eyes growing wide.

"Treasure! Treasure!" said Patty, flapping her wings.

"Better pull it up," said Queen Jennifer, smiling.

Pirate Pete, Olivia and Juniper brushed away the dirt while Queen Jennifer held the lantern so they could see. In the hole was a small wooden chest. It was the size of their picnic basket. It had rope handles on either side.

Olivia expected it to be very heavy, but when she pulled on the handle on the side, it lifted up easily. Still, they worked together to get the chest out of the hole.

"Let's find out what the treasure is," said Pirate Pete. "I hope it's gold coins!"

"I hope it's sparkling gems!" said Olivia.

"I hope it's chocolate!" said Juniper.

Olivia hoped it was not chocolate. If the treasure had been buried for a long time, the chocolate might not taste good.

Pirate Pete opened the chest, and they all leaned forward to look inside. But the only thing they saw was a single piece of paper in the light of Pirate Pete's lantern.

"Arrr," said Pirate Pete. He seemed confused. "Shiver me timbers!"

Juniper and Olivia looked at one another. Then they both whispered, "Pirate-talk!"

Pirate Pete picked up the paper and looked at it. "It must be another clue to where the treasure really is!"

Pete handed the paper to Olivia, who read it out loud.

There is a place where a dragon roams
And unicorns play all day long
There you'll see all sorts of gnomes
And towers tall and strong
Hurry now, and find your way
Through wildflowers of every kind
Quick and go to where I say
And there the treasure you will find

Juniper jumped up and down excitedly. "I know where it is! I know where it is! The treasure is at Wildflower Castle!"

"Yes!" said Olivia. "There are lots of unicorns and wildflowers at Wildflower Castle!"

"But I don't understand this part about the gnomes," said Pirate Pete, scratching his head.

"We did it," said Juniper. "We planted a little garden in the courtyard and put some ceramic gnomes with tall red hats there for decoration."

"Oh, I see," said Pirate Pete. "I'm lucky you two were with me on this treasure hunt! I would never have figured that out on my own."

"Very lucky, indeed," said Queen Jennifer. She was smiling again.

"But how did someone else know about the gnomes?" asked Juniper.

"Yeah, who buried this treasure?" asked Olivia.

"I guess we'll just have to wait and see," said Queen Jennifer, with a twinkle in her eye.

CHAPTER FIVE

TREASURE!

THEY ALL HURRIED from the cave, with Olivia and Juniper running in the front and Patty flying beside them.

"Wait for me!" cried Pirate Pete, who couldn't move as quickly with his wooden peg leg.

"So sorry," said Princess Olivia. The girls slowed down to wait for Pirate Pete to catch up.

To their great surprise, they found King Andrew waiting outside the cave. He was riding on a unicorn, and beside him were three other unicorns, all saddled and ready for riders. The princesses were excited because it was four of their favorite unicorns: Blaze, Mystic, Dreamer, and Stardust.

"Dad!" cried Juniper. "What are you doing here?"

"I thought you might be ready to come back to the castle," he said. "And it's a very long way, so I thought you might want to ride instead of walking. It will be much faster this way, don't you think?"

Olivia put her hands on her hips. "Yes," she said, "but how did you know we were here at the mysterious cave? We were following the treasure map."

King Andrew shrugged and smiled. "Just a lucky guess, I suppose!" And then King Andrew winked at Queen Jennifer.

"Arr," said Pirate Pete. Then he scratched his big red beard. "There seems to be a lot of luck going around today."

Queen Jennifer smiled and laughed a little, but she tried to hide it.

They all got on the unicorns to ride back to the castle. Everyone had their own unicorn except Juniper, who was still too small to ride a unicorn by herself. She and King Andrew rode on Blaze together.

It was still a very pleasant day. The sky was a brilliant blue with a few fluffy clouds drifting lazily across the sky. Earlier, Olivia had thought it was perfect weather for a picnic at the beach, but now she realized it was actually perfect weather for finding a treasure, too.

Everyone was so focused on guiding the unicorns back to the castle that no one noticed the small bag lying in the road, except for Juniper. As only a rider on the unicorn, she looked around more than the others.

"Hold on," Juniper said. "There's something in the road!"

They dismounted their unicorns. Juniper picked up the little bag. It had a little string holding it shut, and so she pulled it open. Inside were many colorful jewels that glowed and sparkled in the bright sunlight.

"Wow!" said Juniper. "It's a treasure!"

"Amazing," said Olivia. "We should split it up, so we can all have a share."

"Split it up! Split it up!" said Patty.

"Now wait a minute," said Pirate Pete. "This isn't the treasure we're looking for. Our treasure is at the castle. This treasure belongs to someone else. Someone probably dropped it here by accident. We should find out who owns it and return it to them."

Olivia and Juniper both realized that Pirate Pete was right, but they hadn't expected a pirate to say something like that. They looked at Pete with curious expressions.

"What's the matter?" asked Pirate Pete. "These are marvelous gems and jewels. Don't you want to help return this to its owner? Whoever it is will be very sad that these jewels and gems are missing!"

"Yes," said Olivia. "You're right. But we thought pirates are always trying to get all the treasure they can."

"Yeah," said Juniper. "Don't pirates steal from other ships and take things that aren't yours?"

Pirate Pete looked shocked. "I would never!"

He shook his head. "Aye, it's true that there are some pirates who might steal and take things that don't belong to them."

"That's not the kind of pirate Pete is," said Queen Jennifer.

"That's right!" said Pirate Pete. Then he laughed. "I'm a pirate because I love sailing on the ocean and looking for lost treasures! It makes me feel great when I return lost treasure to whoever has lost it!"

Olivia and Juniper's eyes got wide and their mouths were open with surprise.

"I guess you could say I'm a peaceful pirate. I help people find things that are lost!"

Olivia and Juniper thought Pirate Pete would be mean and ruthless. They thought he would take things that didn't belong to him. But now they knew better. They had learned a lot of things that day.

"Maybe we shouldn't think we know all about someone until we get to know them," said Olivia.

"Good idea!" said King Andrew.

"We learned lots of things like that today," said Pirate Pete. "Juniper didn't think she'd like going into a mysterious cave. And Olivia didn't think she'd like digging for treasure."

The girls nodded. They were glad they had been willing to get to know Pete and to try new things.

"Now let's find out where this jewelry belongs," said the peaceful Pirate Pete. "We can look for clues and use it like a treasure map."

They looked through the jewelry. There were necklaces and earrings and bracelets.

"Whoever lost this is probably so sad," said Juniper.

"This watch has initials on it," said Olivia. "C.I.S. What does that mean?"

"Oh," said Queen Jennifer, "It must be Countess Ingrid of Sugarland. She often rides her horse on this road. I bet she dropped it."

"Well, let's get it back to her," said Pirate Pete. "We wouldn't want her to worry anymore than she already has."

The group quickly rode to the neighboring village of Sugarland and returned the bag of jewelry to Countess Ingrid.

"Thank you so much," said Countess Ingrid. "These jewels have been in my family for ages. I was taking them to be cleaned by the jewelry maker and didn't realize they had slipped out of my bag! I've been looking everywhere!"

Countess Ingrid handed each of the princesses and Pirate Pete a gold coin to thank them for their help.

"You don't have to give us a reward," said Juniper.

"Yes, we were happy to help," said Olivia.

"I insist," said Countess Ingrid.

CHAPTER SIX

THE BEST TREASURE

Happily putting their gold coins in their pockets, the group made their way back to the unicorns waiting outside.

"I'm glad we helped Countess Ingrid," said Pirate Pete. "It was nice of her to give us a reward. But now I want to find the treasure from Queen Jennifer's map. Finding treasures is my favorite part of being a peaceful pirate."

"Then let's ride quickly," said Queen Jennifer. "I want you to find the treasure, too."

"Let's go! Let's go!" said Patty.

All this talk of treasure seemed to excite the unicorns, too. They galloped even more quickly. And so they all traveled from the sandy beach over rolling green hills. They rode through the forest and past the village and back to Wildflower Castle. The unicorns slowed as they entered the courtyard.

All around were colorful lanterns and banners and streamers. There were balloons and flowers.

"Shiver me timbers!" shouted Pirate Pete. "What a gorgeous sight!"

Everyone from the castle was there and many of the people from the village as well. Miss Beets, the head chef, stood next to a long table that had all kinds of delicious foods. In the middle of the table was an eight-layer cake topped with candles.

"Happy birthday, Pete!" exclaimed Queen Jennifer.

"Oh, what a wonderful surprise!" said Pirate Pete.

"There's no treasure?" asked Juniper.

"We wanted to surprise Pete," said Queen Jennifer. "We knew if we told him there was a treasure map that he would be sure to come visit." She turned to look at Pete. "I'm sorry there's not a real treasure."

"You're wrong about that," said Pirate Pete with a big smile. "Being with people who care about you is the best treasure there is!"

"Best treasure! Best treasure!" squawked Patty.

Everyone laughed.

After a delicious dinner prepared by Miss Beets, it was time for birthday cake. Pirate Pete was a tall fellow, and the cake was nearly as tall as he was! He blew out the candles with one great breath.

Then Miss Beets cut the cake into slices and gave everyone a piece.

Olivia and Juniper sat under a tree with their cake.

"Are you sad we didn't find a real treasure?" Olivia asked Juniper.

Juniper thought about it. "Well," she said. "Maybe I should be sad, but this cake is delicious. We got a gold coin from Countess Ingrid. We got to spend the day with our Uncle Pete, who we didn't know very well before. He is very friendly, and he taught us all about treasure hunting. To me, it feels like we really did find a treasure."

"I like it when things turn out different than you expected, but still very good," said Olivia.

Juniper tried to answer back, but her mouth was full of cake. Olivia couldn't understand her.

"Do you mean you agree?" said Olivia.

Juniper swallowed her cake and said, "Aye!"

They both laughed and then shouted, "Pirate-talk!"

COULD YOU DO ME A FAVOR?

Thank you for reading The Princess and the Pirate. I hope you enjoyed it!

Could you do me a small favor? Would you leave a review of this book with the retailer where it was purchased? Reviews help me to reach new readers. I would really appreciate it!

—A.M. Luzzader

WWW.AMLUZZADER.COM

- blog
- freebies
- newsletter
- contact info

ABOUT THE AUTHOR

A.M. Luzzader is an award-winning children's book author who writes chapter books and middle grade books. She specializes in writing books for preteens including *A Mermaid in Middle Grade and Arthur Blackwood's Scary Stories for Kids who Like Scary Stories*

A.M. decided she wanted to write fun stories for

kids when she was still a kid herself. By the time she was in fourth grade, she was already writing short stories. In fifth grade, she bought a typewriter at a garage sale to put her words into print, and in sixth grade she added illustrations.

Now that she has decided what she wants to be when she grows up, A.M. writes books for kids full time. She was selected as the Writer of the Year in 2019-2020 by the League of Utah Writers.

A.M. is the mother of a 12-year-old and a 15-year-old who often inspire her stories. She lives with her husband and children in northern Utah. She is a devout cat person and avid reader.

A.M. Luzzader's books are appropriate for ages 5-12. Her chapter books are intended for kindergarten to third grade, and her middle grade books are for third grade through sixth grade. Find out more about A.M., sign up to receive her newsletter, and get special offers at her website: www.amluzzader.com.

facebook.com/a.m.luzzader

instagram.com/amluzzader

ABOUT THE ILLUSTRATOR

Anna M. Clark is an artist who loves to draw, tell stories, and buy journals. She has worked as a baker, a math tutor, a security guard, an art teacher, and works now as an illustrator and artist!

She has traveled through Southeast Asia, was born on Halloween (the best holiday ever), and loves to create large chalk art murals. Anna lives with her husband in their cute apartment in Logan, Utah, with their beautiful basil plant.

Explore more of Anna M. Clark's work and her current projects at her website: annamclarkart.com.

OTHER BOOKS BY
A.M. Luzzader

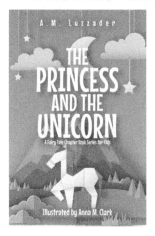 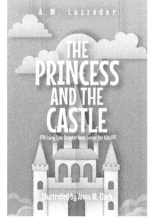

A Fairy Tale Chapter Book Series for Kids

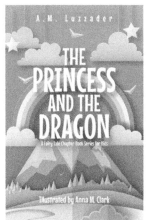

For ages 6-10

OTHER BOOKS BY
A.M. Luzzader

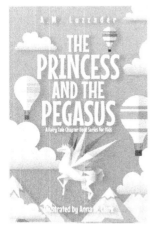

A Fairy Tale Chapter Book Series for Kids

For ages
6-10

OTHER BOOKS BY
A.M. Luzzader

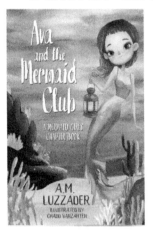 

Mermaid Club: A mermaid girls chapter book

For ages
6-10

OTHER BOOKS BY
A.M. Luzzader

A Magic School for Girls Chapter Book

For ages
6-8

OTHER BOOKS BY
A.M. Luzzader

Decker's Video Game
Rescue Agency

For ages
6-10

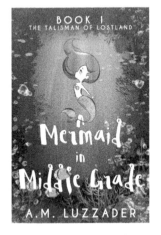 

Hannah Saves the World
Books 1-3

For ages
8-12

Made in the USA
Las Vegas, NV
03 May 2023

71521840R00046